HILDA BOSWELL'S
TREASURY
OF
FAIRY
TALES

LONDON   COLLINS   GLASGOW

ISBN 0 00 137101 0

© COPYRIGHT WM. COLLINS SONS & CO. LTD. 1962

PRINTED AND MADE IN GREAT BRITAIN BY
WILLIAM COLLINS SONS AND CO. LTD.
LONDON AND GLASGOW

CONTENTS

SNOW WHITE and the SEVEN DWARFS

ONCE upon a time in a far-away land there lived a pretty little princess called Snow White. She had a skin as white as snow, hair as black as ebony and lips as red as cherries.

Her mother the Queen had died when she was quite young and some time afterwards her father the King married another wife and brought her to the palace. The new Queen was very beautiful but she was so proud and haughty that she could not bear anyone to be prettier than herself. She owned a wonderful, magic mirror, and when she stepped before it and said:

> " Oh, mirror, mirror, on the wall,
> Who is the fairest of us all? "

it replied:

> " Thou art the fairest, lady Queen."

But little Snow White was growing prettier and prettier

as each day passed, and one day when the Queen spoke to her mirror it made a different answer:

"O Queen, thy loveliness is rare,
    But Snow White seems to all more fair."

The Queen immediately flew into a furious rage and  resolved in her heart that Snow White must die. So she called one of her huntsmen and ordered him to take the little princess into the huge forest which surrounded the palace, and leave her there to die. The huntsman was a kindly man and was most unwilling to do this cruel deed, but he was too afraid of the Queen to disobey her commands.

He took Snow White into the for-est, but instead of

leaving her in the heart of the dense woods, he took her to a part which was not so thickly wooded and left her there.

Poor little Snow White was very frightened alone in the woods. Darkness was falling and although she was not in the thickest part of the wood, she was still lost, lonely and afraid. She started to run blindly between the tall trees and just when she felt that she couldn't go on any farther, she came upon a clearing where there stood a little cottage.

Snow White tapped timidly on the cottage door to ask

for shelter for the night, but no one came. She knocked again a bit louder but still there was no reply. Eventually she pushed the door cautiously and found that it was not locked. Inside, the cottage was small but very clean and tidy. There was a table neatly set with seven little plates, seven little knives and seven little forks. Beside the fire were seven little chairs and on the other side by the wall were seven little beds.

Snow White was hungry so she ate some bread from each of the little plates, and then she felt so sleepy that she lay down on one of the little beds. Immediately she fell fast asleep, and didn't even wake when the owners of the cottage came home.

They were seven little dwarfs who dug for ore all day in the mountains. Every night they came home to their cottage in the wood, tired and hungry, looking forward to a meal and a long sleep.

They were angry when they discovered that someone had come into their cottage while they were out, and even angrier to find that some bread had been eaten from each of their plates. But when they came upon Snow White sleeping peacefully in one of their beds they could not be angry any longer for they had never seen such a beautiful girl in all their lives before. They shook her gently to awaken her, and when she told them about how the wicked Queen had tried to kill her, they felt very sorry and said she might stay with them for as long as she wanted.

"You can wash our clothes, and cook our food and clean our cottage," they told her, "but you must remember that while we are away in the mountains all day, you must not let *anyone* in the cottage. For if your wicked

stepmother finds out that you still live, she may try to harm you again."

Snow White loved keeping house for the seven dwarfs and for a long time she lived happily with them, always remembering never to let anyone come into the cottage. But one day she was feeling rather bored and when an old woman came to the door selling apples, she forgot the dwarfs' warning, and asked her to come in. "For what harm can an old woman do to me?" thought Snow White.

But Snow White did not know that the old woman was none other than her wicked stepmother in disguise. The Queen had discovered from the magic mirror that Snow White was not dead but was living with the dwarfs in the forest. Immediately she had started to make plans, wondering how she could get rid of her stepdaughter. At last she had had an idea. She would poison an apple, disguise herself as an old woman and take the apple to Snow White. She chose a lovely shining, rosy-red apple which she knew the Princess would be unable to resist, and set off for the cottage in the forest.

Snow White accepted the apple with delight, and it looked so fresh and rosy that she took a great bite from it. Immediately she fell down, as though she were dead, and the wicked Queen went away, laughing gleefully because her plans had gone so well.

When the dwarfs came home at the

end of the day, they were heartbroken to see Snow White lying so still and so white on the floor.

"We cannot bury her in the cold ground," said one.

"Oh, no!" the rest of them chorused.

"Let us make a glass case," said another. "We shall place her in it and everyone who passes may see the beautiful princess."

The dwarfs all agreed to do this and set about building a beautiful glass case. This done, they laid Snow White in it very tenderly, and carried it to the top of a high hill.

Some time after, a Prince was riding by and when he saw Snow White he immediately fell deeply in love with her. He begged the dwarfs to let him take her back to his Palace with him, and when they realised how much he loved their dear Snow White, they agreed.

They helped the Prince to carry the glass case back to his Palace, but going along a rough track, one of the dwarfs stumbled and the case was jolted. At once the piece of poisoned apple fell from Snow White's mouth.

She opened her eyes and, raising the lid of the glass case, she sat up and smiled at them all.

The Prince and the dwarfs were overjoyed to see her alive and well, and the Prince asked her to honour him by becoming his wife. Snow White consented because she loved the Prince on sight, and the Prince promised that the dwarfs would be looked after all their lives.

So everyone lived happily ever after—everyone, that is, but the wicked Queen who was banished from the kingdom for ever.

The Babes in the Wood

OLD GREY OWL had just woken up. He was flitting silently from branch to branch, looking for his supper, and most of the other creatures in the forest had begun to settle for their night's sleep, when they heard a terrible noise. The robins, blackbirds and thrushes lifted their sleepy heads from their nests and listened; the baby fawn crept closer to his mother in the bracken; the squirrels whisked their tails in the air; and the rabbits, who were playing a last game of "Poor Bunny sits a-weeping," scuttered away.

Crashing their way through the forest strode two fierce men, dragging with them a little boy and girl. As they came into the clearing the men stopped, and threw the children to the ground.

"No one will ever find them here," said one, and with the huge sacks of treasure, which the robbers had stolen from the children's father, they made off.

All the creatures of the forest stayed very quiet and still until the last sound of the trampling of leaves and the snapping of twigs had died away. Then a little robin

flew down and took a good look at the children, who were doing their best to comfort each other.

"It's children! That's what it is!" chirped Robin.

"How do you know?" asked Squirrel, scornfully.

"Do-oo you-oo? Do-oo you-oo?" cooed the wood pigeons.

The baby fawn stayed close by his mother and the forest creatures watched and waited until the two children, worn out with crying, fell asleep in each other's arms. Then one by one the animals crept closer.

"Poor little things!" said the fawn's mother, her big brown eyes full of sorrow.

"They ought to be safe in their nests at this time of night," said one of the blackbirds.

"Do-oo something!" cooed the wood pigeons.

The rabbits and the squirrels were too busy to talk, for they were scurrying about collecting the dry fallen leaves and heaping them over the two children.

"They'll be nice and warm now," said a rabbit.

"Won't they be hungry when they wake up?" whispered the baby fawn.

All the other creatures rushed about finding food for the children. The squirrels brought nuts, the birds brought berries, and Robin told them which ones would be safe for children to eat. Even Old Grey Owl went back to his house in the tree and came out with two dead mice, which made the others laugh; except of course old Grandfather Fieldmouse, who was simply furious.

Then Robin said: "As soon as it is light I shall fly off. I shan't come back until I've found someone who will take care of these children."

"That's all very well," said Old Grey Owl, "but how can you tell them that children are here?"

"Pooh!" said Robin. "Leave that to me!" And, flying down from his branch, he tweaked a button from the little boy's coat.

"Won't do-ooo! Won't do-ooo!" cooed the pigeon sadly.

Then Squirrel frisked down the tree. He nibbled the

little girl's hair-ribbon with his sharp teeth till he had cut right through and then, with a smart bow, he handed the tiny piece to the robin.

Very early in the morning, when the trees still looked grey and misty, Robin set out. The blue ribbon was knotted carefully round his neck, and in his beak he carried the bright, shiny button. At last he came to the edge of the forest and to the cottage where the old woman who put out crumbs and fresh water for him, lived by herself. Robin perched on a branch by the cottage door and sang his sweetest and loudest.

"Bless me!" cried the old woman. "There's my friend!" And she opened the little door and peeped out. How she laughed when she saw that Robin was wearing a blue silk neck-tie!

Robin flew down, and dropped the bright, shiny button at her feet, and as she stooped to pick it up, the old woman saw that it was the button she herself had sewn on the little coat she had made for her grandson.

"Bless me!" said the old woman. She looked again at the robin and saw that the neck-tie he was wearing was a piece of the very hair-ribbon she herself had bought from the pedlar for her little granddaughter.

Robin flew a little way off, and sang again, his loudest and clearest, and the old woman wrapped her shawl round her shoulders and followed him; and so they came at last to the children, Robin always leading the way, waiting and singing on bush after bush until the old woman had caught up with him.

"Bless me!" cried the old woman, when she saw her two little grand-children.

"Oh, Grannie!" said the little boy. "We had such a horrid dream—all about robbers."

"Bless me!" she said. "That is over now."

She sounded so kind that none of the forest creatures felt afraid of her, and they all drew near.

"It is such a long way to my cottage," she said.

"Then the children shall ride on my back," said the fawn's mother.

All the way, the fawn skipped by his mother's side, and the rabbits and squirrels followed after; and over their heads flew the singing birds. When they came to the cottage the old woman went to her cupboard and brought out the nicest things she could find, and they all sat down in the little garden and had a grand feast.

"Bless me!" said the old woman. "It's just like a party!"

The Pied Piper

THIS is the story of a strange thing that happened six hundred years ago in the old German town of Hamelin.

Hamelin was a pleasant place. The old houses had crooked gables and leaned across the cobbled streets. The spires of churches rose high above the tiled roofs, and outside the wall of the town flowed the broad, shining river. Many children lived in Hamelin and ran to and fro over the cobblestones, shouting and laughing. The little boys had rosy cheeks and the little girls had curls as fair as flax.

But one year the happy town found itself troubled by a great host of rats who had travelled from—nobody knew where. What was worse—nobody could think how to get rid of them. Brown rats, grey rats, black rats, solemn old rats with whiskers, frisky young rats with long tails; they ran about all over Hamelin, scratching behind walls, running pitter-pat up and down stairs and in and out of kitchens, squeaking in their hundreds so that people could not hear themselves speak. They killed all the Hamelin cats and fought the dogs quite boldly. They were too cunning to be caught in traps. What could be done?

At last the Hamelin people grew very angry and flocked to the Town Hall where the Mayor of Hamelin and his Aldermen, dressed in their crimson gowns, sat at a long table talking about the rats. RATS. This was all anybody could think about.

" Ah ! " shouted the Hamelin people. " Why do we have a Mayor and Aldermen ? Why do we buy them crimson gowns lined with ermine ? They can't even rid us of a plague of rats ! " And as they grew more angry, they shouted, " If you don't hurry up and do something we'll get rid of *you* ! "

The fat old Mayor of Hamelin scratched his head and all the Aldermen looked terribly worried.

"What *can* we do?" they muttered to one another, but nobody had a single useful idea, and when they heard a light rap on the door of the Town Hall they jumped quite nervously because they thought it was a *rat* scratching at the door. "Tap, tap!" they heard again, and the Mayor, trying to look bold, called out: "Come in!"

The door opened. Somebody came in. The Mayor and his Aldermen stared and stared in wonderment, their eyes big with surprise. Such a queer fellow stepped softly into the Town Hall. He was tall and thin, his skin dark and his hair very light. He had greeny-blue eyes that glinted like the point of a new pin and little smiles played about his lips. But his coat made them stare most of all.

It was very long and covered him from top to toe.   Half the coat was red and the other half a gay yellow.

This queer stranger walked up to the Mayor's table and said :

" Please, your honours, I know a charm that will make any living creature follow me.   Whether they creep, or fly, or run, or swim, I can charm them.   In my time I have travelled to many kingdoms.   They call me the Pied Piper."

Still staring with all their eyes, the Mayor and Corporation noticed a pipe hanging at the end of the stranger's scarf.   (He had a gaily-striped scarf of red and yellow to match his coat.)   They noticed that his fingers touched his dangling pipe as if they simply itched to play it, and before they could speak the Piper said :

" If I get rid of your rats, will you pay me a thousand guilders ? "

" *Fifty* thousand ! " shouted the delighted Mayor and all the Aldermen together.

Then the Piper stepped softly into the street, his eyes sparkling greeny-blue, a wise little smile curling his lips as he lifted his magic pipe. He blew three shrill notes, and at once, pitter-patter ! pitter-patter ! on the cobblestones came the sound of the rats running and frisking and hurrying to follow the Pied Piper playing his sweet tune. On he walked towards the walls of the town, piping gaily as he walked, and the pattering noise grew louder until it swelled to a rumble as rats, brown and grey and black, old and young, came tumbling in hundreds and thousands out of the old gabled houses. The Mayor and

Aldermen stood staring from the doors of the Town Hall; people in their doorways stared with eyes and mouths wide open in wonder. Still the Piper walked on, playing his pipe, and still the rats followed. At last, Piper and rats reached the river outside the walls, and at once the rats plunged in, never to be seen again.

All except one. One stout old grey rat swam the broad river and reached the far side. Very scared, he scurried off to Ratland and told the tribe of rats who lived there the very strangest story.

"I heard the clear notes of a pipe," he said, "and at once I could hear people opening cupboards full of jams and pickles. I could hear the people opening casks of butter and barrels of sugar. Then I heard a voice cry; 'Rats, munch and crunch as much as you wish!' and the next moment—splash! I found myself in the river!"

You can imagine that all the rats declared none of them would ever go to Hamelin.

In Hamelin, the people were ringing all the church bells so joyfully that all the steeples rocked above the roof-tops! The fat old Mayor stood beaming in the market-place, shouting: "Now be sure you fill up every rat-hole in Hamelin! Don't leave one!" But suddenly, his beaming face grew long and doleful as a tall thin fellow, in a coat of red and yellow, leaped up in front of him as swiftly as a candle-flame. It was the Pied Piper!

"Please, pay me my thousand guilders!" he said.

A thousand guilders! The Mayor looked very glum and muttered to the Aldermen who also looked glum and muttered something in reply. Pay a thousand guilders to a wandering gipsy dressed in red and yellow! Why, a thousand guilders would pay for a splendid banquet for the Mayor and Aldermen! "Besides," whispered the Mayor, winking at the Aldermen, "those rats are drowned! He can't bring them back!"

All this time the Pied Piper waited patiently, fingering his pipe as he stood in the market-place. The Mayor turned to him and said, "You know we were only joking when we promised a thousand guilders. Come now, we'll give you fifty."

A dark frown chased the smile from the Piper's face.

"Keep your promise," he said to the Mayor. "If you cheat, I'll play another tune that you won't like!"

The Mayor's face turned red with rage.

"You impudent fellow!" he shouted. "Go on, blow your pipe till you burst!"

The Mayor and Aldermen and townspeople of Hamelin stood laughing at the Piper as he stepped out of the market-place. He looked very serious, but he said nothing. He just lifted his pipe to his lips and blew three long sweet notes, clear as a bird's. The Mayor and people stared in wonderment, then a look of horror came over every face as they watched the Piper walk down the street, piping as he stepped. For the street had filled with a rustling, pattering, chattering noise, the sound of dancing feet and happy voices and clapping hands. The children of Hamelin came skipping and running, their wooden shoes

clattering on the cobblestones as they followed the Pied Piper. On they ran, talking and singing, little boys with red cheeks and little girls with flaxen curls.

But the Mayor and Aldermen and all the grown-ups of Hamelin stood as still as stones and could not speak a word. With beating hearts they watched the children follow the Piper through the winding streets away from the town. He did not lead them towards the river, but towards the mountain that rose high and blue above the west wall. The people said to themselves : " Oh, the Piper can't climb the mountain. He'll stop piping and let the children return."

But no !   The Piper and his procession reached the mountain and at once a door opened in the mountain-side to let the Piper and the dancing children pass through. Then the door closed; the piping and the laughter died away.   All the children of Hamelin had gone.

No, not all.   One little lame boy, who could not run so fast, turned back to Hamelin.   His parents ran to meet him, weeping for joy.   But the little boy looked sad.   He told them that when he first heard the sweet notes of the magic pipe he heard the music calling children to a lovely country where the flowers had colours never dreamed of in Hamelin, where sparrows had gay feathers like those of peacocks, and the horses flew on wings.   Nobody in that country was sad or lame or tired.

When he grew up, this little boy told his grandchildren how his playmates all went away one day with the Pied Piper and left him behind.   And he showed them the window in one of the Hamelin churches where, painted in colours on the glass, children followed the Pied Piper in his long coat of red and yellow.

Tom Thumb

AN old man and his wife sat by the open window of their cottage one summer's evening.

" It is getting too dark to see," said the old man. " Time to go to bed."

" I have just finished. What do you think of this? " said his wife, and she held up a baby's bonnet, beautifully worked with fine, small stitches.

" It is well done," said the old man; " but you know it would give me real pleasure if it could have been for our own child."

The old woman sighed, for she had always wanted children of her very own. Instead she spent her time in sewing pretty things for every new baby who came to the village.

" Yes," she said now, " I should have been happy, too,

if we had even only one child; even if it should be as small as my thumb."

Outside the window they heard a peal of silvery laughter.

"That wasn't a bird," said the old man. "Come to bed, wife!" So they closed the window and went upstairs.

The fairy, for it was a fairy who had heard them talking, flew back to fairyland and told the Queen about the little old woman who would welcome a baby no bigger than her thumb.

"If she is a good woman she shall have her child," said the Queen, and waved her magic wand.

The next morning, when the old woman woke, there beside her lay the most perfect little boy she had ever seen. He had bright, brown eyes and a mop of curly

hair, and he lay there chuckling and laughing, as merry as could be . . . and he was exactly the size of the old woman's thumb! She was overjoyed, and now busied herself in making the tiniest and finest baby clothes anyone had ever seen. The baby was so small that she made him a cradle from a pea-pod, and lined it each day with fresh flower petals.

They were poor old people, but she had saved for years the small scraps left over from the sewing she had done for others, and now all these were put to good use, and Tom Thumb, for that was his name, was finely dressed. The old woman even used rose petals to line his cloth bonnets, and plaited fine grasses to make shoes for his small feet.

Everyone came from miles around to see this little boy, who never grew any bigger. He could sing and talk, though his voice was no louder than that of a mouse, and he was full of fun, but the school-mistress found she could not have him in school, for when he was there the children never did any lessons! Tom Thumb would sit in a little box on the teacher's desk, and whenever her back was turned, he would balance on the ink-well or slide down the ruler and make the children laugh!

He kept the old man and woman very busy, for he was always up to tricks, and he was so tiny that he could hide in all sorts of small corners. They often lost sight of him for hours at a time. Sometimes he was allowed to go farther from home in the old man's pocket, and then his mother would dress Tom Thumb in a scarlet coat and cap, so that he could be more easily seen, if he strayed.

One day the old man went fishing, and Tom Thumb begged to go too.

"Very well," said his mother; "but be a good boy and stay close to your father, or a big fish will swallow you up."

"Even a little fish could swallow Tom Thumb," laughed the old man, as they set off. He was so busy with his work, and so un-used to having Tom Thumb with him by the river-side, that the old man soon forgot all about him, and it was not until it was time to return home that he dis-covered there was no sign any-where of little Tom Thumb.

He called and called, and he searched until it was almost too dark to see his way home, but he could find no trace of him—not even his scarlet cap.

Sadly he returned to the old woman, who had a fine supper waiting, and was ready to scold him for keeping the little boy out so late, but when she saw that he came alone she burst into tears.

"I expect the fairies took him. He must have been a gift from the fairies in the first place, and I suppose they have taken him back," said the old man.

"No! No!" cried the old woman. "You forgot him. I know you did. And poor Tom Thumb has fallen into the river and been swallowed by a fish."

The old woman was right, for Tom had gone off to explore the river's bank, and, slipping in the mud, had fallen in, and almost at once had been swallowed by an

enormous fish. It was very dark and warm inside, but Tom was not uncomfortable and he soon fell asleep.

Now this fish was so *enormous* that the man who caught it said to himself: " A splendid fish indeed! Good enough for the King! And as he was passing that way, he called in at the Palace and gave it to the Royal cook.

Tom Thumb did not wake up until the fish, coated with shrimp sauce and trimmed with lemon and parsley, was set before the King on a silver dish, and then, as the fish was cut open, he sat up, feeling very hot and stuffy, and red in the face, and waved his cap.

" Hey, there! What are you doing, waking me up like that? " shouted Tom, and the King and Queen and all the Lords and Ladies burst out laughing at the sight of the comical little fellow. The King set him on the rim of his wine-glass, and fed him dainty morsels on the end of a pin, and let him dance about the table, and swing from the flowers. Tom, who was never shy, had a splendid time, and was quite content to stay in the Palace as long as people were kind to him.

The King had a special little chair made for him, from solid silver, with tiny red velvet cushions, and Tom sat in this chair, close to the King's plate, at every meal. He had a little house of his own, like a doll's house, only much finer, in the Palace grounds, and the furniture in it was copied from the Queen's own designs. Tom wore clothes of satin and velvet and even carried a tiny golden sword—not that it was sharp enough to cut anything—for the King was afraid Tom might hurt himself. For a time Tom was very happy, but he soon found that the King treated him as a toy; like a little clown who could be wound up, to hop and skip and dance, and to make people laugh.

It was very tiring trying to keep the King and Queen amused. Tom did not like it when the ladies of the Court picked him up and petted him as though he were some sort of small, tame animal; they even knelt down on the grass before the windows of his little house

and peeped in at him; and once when he had drawn the curtains, the Queen was very angry. So poor Tom began to wish he could be back in the cottage with his own mother and father.

He grew pale and thin, and did not laugh or sing or dance any more, and he tried hard to think of some way in which he could get back home again.

One day the King said to the Queen: "I am tired of the little fellow. He has grown very dull. What shall we do with him?"

The Queen thought for a long while, and then she said:

" I think the best thing would be to give him to some
kind country folk to care for. We could pay them
well, of course."

" Good! " said the King. " Then we could have him
at the Palace on special occasions; that would be far
more amusing than seeing him every day."

Tom began to cheer up when he heard this, and he
jumped out of the Queen's wardrobe, where he had been
hiding, and danced all about the room.

" Oh, so you have heard, have you? " laughed the
King. " Very well, little fellow, you shall have one
wish before you leave the Palace."

The Queen sighed, thinking that Tom, who was by
this time very spoilt, would be sure to choose something
like a dozen servants, or a bag of diamonds. She was so
surprised and pleased when Tom said:

" I should like to go home."

The King was pleased, too, and he had all Tom's things carefully packed and went himself to the cottage of the old man and his wife, who were so very happy to see Tom again that they gladly forgave him for staying away so long. They agreed to take Tom to the Palace twice a year on the King's and the Queen's birthdays, and to take great care of him for the rest of his life.

The old man and woman were never tired of hearing of Tom's adventures, and each time he returned he had fresh things to tell them, so they were never dull, and they all lived happily together in the little cottage.

The Brave Little Tailor

EARLY one morning, a tiny, crooked little tailor called Hans sat sewing in his workroom. He was stitching away very busily at a silk waistcoat and had not found time to have any breakfast. It was dark in his workroom, so Hans had pushed the table into the window and perched himself on top of the table to sew. He could see his stitches better like this, and he could look out now and then at people passing in the busy street.

All at once Hans heard a voice calling loudly down the street :

" Honey for sale ! Buy my fine honey ! "

This made Hans lay down his sewing and put his head out of the window to find out who was crying, " Buy my fine honey ! " He saw a plump market-woman in a red cloak walking along the street and carrying on her arm a basket that held a dozen pots of honey.

"Come this way!" cried the little tailor. "I will buy your honey."

The market-woman came bustling down the street and stood smiling outside the tailor's window. But when he held out a plate and spoon and said humbly, "I will buy four ounces," she stopped smiling and tossed her head as she measured out the honey and took the tailor's pennies.

"I thought you would buy several pots," she said, and turned away to find another customer. But Hans got out his loaf from a cupboard, cut a big slice and spread it with honey.

"Bread and honey for breakfast! It will be a treat," he said to himself. "But first I will finish my seam."

So he laid his slice of bread-and-honey on the table and went on sewing. A few minutes later he laid down his work and turned round to pick up the slice of bread.

As he did so, a crowd of flies buzzed through the open window. They had smelt the honey and wanted to taste it.

"You were not invited! Leave my breakfast alone!" shouted the tailor angrily, as he picked up a piece of cloth and struck at the flies. Seven flies lay dead upon the table.

"What a brave fellow I am!" exclaimed the foolish little tailor. "It is time everybody knew about the Brave Little Tailor who lives in this town!"

Quickly he found a piece of black cloth and cut himself a belt. He took a needle and a length of scarlet thread and made big letters in scarlet stitching all round the belt.

"Seven at one stroke," spelt the letters on the belt. Proudly the tailor fastened the belt round his waist.

"I'm going out into the world to let people know how brave I am," he said. Before saying good-bye to the little boy in the back room who was his apprentice, he

looked in his cupboard but could find nothing except a cheese which he stuffed into his pocket. Outside the door he saw a bird fluttering in a bush. He caught the bird and hid it in another pocket. Then he set off.

Hans, the tailor, walked a long way. Later in the day he found himself on top of a mountain where, right in the middle of the road, a giant

sat resting with his huge brown hands clasped around his knees. He could have picked up the tailor easily in two of his great brown fingers, but Hans, the tailor, strutted up to him quite boldly and said :

" Sir, I am out in search of adventure. Shall we travel together ? "

The giant blinked his eyes in surprise at the tiny tailor who was not as tall as the giant's knee and answered in a rumbling voice : " You conceited little fellow ! You are no bigger than a grasshopper. What use would you be as my companion ? "

" Read this, " replied Hans proudly, and unbuttoned his coat to show the giant his belt. The giant bent down to read the letters stitched in red.

" Seven at one stroke, " he read. At once the giant looked more respectful. " Whoever would believe it ? " he said. " You are a tiny little fellow to kill seven men at

one stroke. How brave you are ! But I am sure you cannot do *this.*" The giant stooped down to pick up a big stone and squeezed the stone in his huge brown fist until water ran from it.

"That is nothing," replied Hans. "I can do it quite easily." He took the soft cheese from his pocket and squeezed it till the whey dripped from it.

The giant looked astonished.

"But you can't do *this*, can you ?" he said, picking up another big stone and tossing it high in the air. His strong arm flung the stone so high that they could not see where it fell.

"You can throw well," said the tailor, "but your stone has fallen somewhere. Now *I* can throw a stone so high that it will *never* come down again."

"Nonsense ! " cried the giant.

But the tailor put his hand into his other pocket, drew out the bird, and threw it up into the air. The joyous bird took wing and soared out of sight into the blue sky.

"You *are* a strong fellow!" said the giant in admiration. "Come along home with me and meet my brothers."

Luckily for Hans, the tailor, the giant had walked a hundred miles that day and now felt tired, so he walked very slowly. By running as fast as his short legs could go the little tailor managed to keep up with the giant, but he was glad when they came to a great spreading cherry tree loaded with black cherries and the giant said:

"Little man, I'll reach some cherries for you to eat."

The giant reached up to the top branch of the tree, pulled it downwards and said:

"Hold this in your hand and eat the cherries."

The tailor took the branch

in his hand, but he had not enough strength to hold it. The branch of cherries sprang back into the air while the little tailor, very frightened, clung on with both hands. But the branch of cherries dipped down again on the other side of the tree and the nimble tailor dropped lightly to the ground.

" Ha, ha, ha ! " laughed the giant. " You call yourself a strong man, you say you can kill seven at one stroke, yet you haven't the strength to hold on to a twig like that ! "

" Nonsense," replied the tailor. " I sprang right over the cherry tree. *You* are not strong enough to do that."

The huge clumsy giant took a leap at the tree, but he could not jump over and got tangled in its branches. The little tailor stood roaring with laughter beneath the tree.

" I am stronger than you ! " he cried.

At last the giant managed to climb down and led the
tailor to his home.   He lived in a cavern in the mountain-
side, and the cavern seemed very dark to the little tailor.
But at the far end he saw a huge red fire flickering, and
near the fire sat two other giants, warming their feet
(in enormous boots) at the roaring flames.   Each giant
was eating a sheep roasted in front of the fire, and each
held a great knife that flashed like a sword in the firelight.
The tailor did not like the look of those giants at all and
hid trembling behind the first giant.

   " Where's *my* supper ? " growled the first giant,
striding up to the fire, and as the giants started to quarrel,
the little tailor ran away very fast down the mountain-
side. He wandered many miles that night, and the next
morning he walked farther until he came to the courtyard
of a palace. It was still very early : everyone in the palace

slept. So the little tailor lay down by the gates to sleep.

As he slept, people began to go in and out of the courtyard, all of them staring in curiosity at the little man who lay there fast asleep with the soles of his boots almost worn through. Then somebody bent over the tailor to take a closer look at the cloth belt he wore, with letters stitched upon it in red.

"Seven at one stroke," they read.

"This must be a hero

from a far country," said one of the King's soldiers. " Send a messenger to the King."

So a messenger hurried to the King and the King sent for the tailor.

" You are a great hero if you can kill seven at one stroke," said the King. " I wish my Generals were as bold."

" Let me enlist in your service, your Majesty," said the tailor boldly. " Then you will not need to fear your enemies."

The King gave the little

tailor a sword and a red coat embroidered with gold. All his Generals had to show great respect to the tiny man who could kill seven at one stroke. But they all grew very tired of hearing the little tailor boast about his deeds of bravery and told the King they wanted to leave his service.

"I almost wish I could send that little man away," thought the King.

One day he called the tailor and said to him: "On the edge of my kingdom there live three giants who rob and kill so that people go in fear of their lives. Rid the kingdom of these giants and you shall marry the Princess and rule over half my kingdom. A hundred knights shall ride with you."

"I shan't need their help!" said the tailor boldly.

Early one morning, the tailor rode out on a little pony at the head of a hundred knights mounted on their prancing steeds. They all laughed at the tiny man who could not have ridden a spirited horse if he tried, and they laughed even more when they saw that he carried a bundle of hay for his pony's fodder. But they were very glad when he told them to wait at the foot of the mountain and rode on up the mountain by himself.

"I killed seven at one stroke!" boasted the tailor. "So I am sure I can kill three giants."

When he came to the cherry tree he tied up his pony to the tree then crept on up the mountainside carrying his bundle of hay. He came to the top of the mountain and saw black smoke curling from a big hole in the ground.

This smoke came from the great fire that burned on the floor of the giants' cave. The tailor stuffed his bundle of hay into the hole and hid himself among the rocks till evening when a grumbling and rumbling inside the

mountain told him the giants were at home, talking together as they ate their supper of roasted sheep. Soon the grumbling and rumbling grew louder. The little tailor could hear stamping and shouting as the giants quarrelled, and then he heard *gigantic* sneezes that made the mountain tremble. As he guessed, the giants' cave had filled with black smoke that came pouring down the chimney and made them sneeze and cough so much that they could not eat a mouthful !

At last the three giants came out of the cave, fighting and quarrelling. He heard the eldest giant shout :

" I know a much more comfortable cave than this about five hundred miles away ! "

Then off they strode, down the mountainside.

The little tailor ran into the cave and found the three huge knives they had left behind in their hurry. He tied a rope around them, dragged them out of the cave, and, with great difficulty, hoisted them on to his pony's back.

" Here are the giants' swords ! " cried the little tailor as he rode back to join the hundred knights.

" He is a hero ! He has killed three giants ! " said the knights.

So the Brave Little Tailor married the proud Princess and ruled over half the kingdom.

One night, however, a curious thing happened. As her husband lay sleeping the Princess heard him talking in his sleep and this is what he said :

" Boy, hurry up and sew these buttons on. I must get this waistcoat finished by eight o'clock."

The Princess told this to her father, the King, who was very angry when he knew that a little tailor had deceived him by calling himself a hero.

" To-night," said the King, " my seven trusty guards shall bind the tailor while he sleeps and put him on a ship for a strange country."

Alarmed for her husband's safety, the Princess told the tailor what the King had said.

" I'll get the better of them ! " said Hans the tailor, bravely enough.

He lay down in bed that night and pretended to sleep soundly. The seven royal guards stood just outside the door and listened to the tailor again talking in his sleep.

"I killed seven at one stroke," said the tailor, in his sleep (so they thought). "One stroke will kill the seven who wait outside my door."

Then the seven tall guards ran away and told the King that they were sure the tiny man who had married the Princess was indeed a great hero and stronger than any of them.

RAPUNZEL

THERE was once, long ago, a beautiful girl called Rapunzel who had long golden hair which she wore in a long plait. When Rapunzel was a baby a wicked witch had stolen her from her mother and father and had shut her up in a tower which stood in a wood. It had neither staircase nor doors, but only a little window high up in the wall.

When the witch wanted

to enter the tower, she stood at the foot of it and shouted:

" Rapunzel, Rapunzel,
let down your hair."

Then Rapunzel would let down her long golden plait and the witch would climb up by it and go in through the window.

Rapunzel was very lonely all day in the tower and often she would sing a plaintive song to pass away the time. One day a Prince rode by the tower and heard her sweet song. Immediately he fell in love with her beautiful voice and made up his mind that some day he would marry the lady who could sing like that. But although he longed to meet her, he could see no way of getting into the tower.

" There's no door and no staircase," he thought to himself sadly, and he rode away through the forest again.

But the voice of Rapunzel haunted the

Prince and every day he rode back to the tower to hear it. One day while he was hiding behind some trees, he saw the witch approach. He saw her come to the foot of the tower and heard her cry:

" Rapunzel, Rapunzel,
   let down your hair."

Then he watched in amazement as Rapunzel lowered her hair from the window and the witch climbed up.
   Next day he rode to the tower, as it began to grow dark, and called softly:

" Rapunzel, Rapunzel,
   let down your hair."

Down came Rapunzel's golden plait and the King's son climbed up by it.

At first Rapunzel was frightened, but the Prince talked to her so kindly that she soon lost her fear. He told her that he had fallen in love with her and wanted to marry her.

" But how can I get down from this tower? " asked poor Rapunzel.

" Next time I come I will bring a rope," said the Prince. " Do not despair. I will help you down and my horse can carry both of us away to my palace where the witch will never find us."

Now Rapunzel's song was happy as she waited and watched for her Prince to come back. But alas, the wicked witch had seen the Prince leave the tower and guessed that

he was planning to take Rapunzel away.

She flew into a furious rage and when she got into the tower she cut off Rapunzel's beautiful hair with an enormous pair of scissors.

"You will never see your fine Prince again!" she shouted at the poor girl.

Then she sent Rapunzel away into the dark forest and she herself hid in the tower until the Prince returned.

When she heard him call:

"Rapunzel, Rapunzel, let down your hair,"

she threw down one end of the long plait while she held the other tightly.

The Prince climbed up the rope, but instead of seeing the beautiful Rapunzel waiting for him at the top, he saw the face of the ugly old witch.

"Ah," she cried mockingly, "you have come to fetch Rapunzel, but you will never see her again."

The Prince was beside himself with grief and in his despair he sprang out of the window. At the foot of the tower was a thorny bush and as the Prince landed on it the thorns hurt his eyes and he became blind.

But he couldn't believe that his lovely Rapunzel was dead and, although he could not see, he set out to search for her. Day

after day he rode in the forest, asking people if they had seen a beautiful fair lady. But no one had.

Then one day as he sat resting in the shade of a large tree, he heard a voice singing. The Prince raised his head, then got up, turning from one side to another to find out from which direction the sound was coming.

For the song was none other than the same sad song

that he had heard Rapunzel sing in the tower. And he knew, without a doubt, that the singer could only be his own dear Rapunzel.

He began to call her name: " Rapunzel! Rapunzel! "

Rapunzel had been living in the forest in great poverty but she thought constantly of her handsome Prince and wondered what had become of him. When she heard his voice calling her name she ran towards the sound and soon

saw her Prince whom she had despaired of ever seeing
again.

She ran to him and threw her arms around his neck.
When she discovered that he was blind, she wept and two
of her tears fell on his eyes.

Immediately his eyes became better and he could see
again.

Then the Prince took Rapunzel away from the forest,
riding his great, white, galloping horse. They rode away
to the Prince's own kingdom where they were received
with joy, and they lived long and happily together.

The WILD SWANS

IN a far-off country dwelt a King who had eleven sons and one daughter, a beautiful child called Elise. The children loved each other and were very happy until the day came when their father, the King, married a very wicked Queen. She sent Elise off into the country to be brought up by peasants, and told the King so many falsehoods about the poor Princes that he took no more interest in them and allowed her to drive them from the palace.

"Go out into the world!" she cried after them. "Go in the form of great speechless birds!"

Immediately the brothers changed into eleven beautiful white swans which flew off above the tree-tops.

Time passed, and when Elise was fifteen years old the King asked for her to return home. When the Queen saw how beautiful she was, she was filled with hatred, and before presenting her to the King, she smeared the maiden's face with walnut juice until it looked quite swarthy, and so entangled her hair that the King was shocked to see such an ugly creature and swore it could not be his daughter.

Poor Elise crept away into the forest and wept; and thought of her eleven brothers. Then she bathed in a nearby stream so that she regained her former beauty.

In the forest she met an old woman. Elise asked her if she had seen eleven princes ride through the wood. "No," replied the old woman, "but I saw eleven swans with gold crowns on their heads." And she took Elise to the place where she had seen the strange birds. Elise thanked the old woman and settled down to wait. Then, just as the sun was sinking, the eleven swans appeared, flying one behind the other. They came to rest beside Elise and flapped their long white wings. As the sun sank behind the trees the swans disappeared and in their place stood the eleven brothers.

"When the sun is above the horizon," explained the eldest brother, "we are swans; but as soon as it sets we regain our human form." The princes now lived in a far-off land, and they began to make plans to

take their sister back with them.

In the morning, when they were once again transformed into birds, the eleven brothers placed Elise on a mat which they had woven during the night from willow bark, and taking the four corners in their beaks, they flew away with her across the sea.

At last they reached the kingdom where the brothers lived, and they took her to a cave where she might sleep comfortably after her long journey. As she slept she had a strange dream. She dreamt that a fairy came and told her how she might free her brothers from the wicked spell.

" But," said the fairy, " you must have courage and patience. Do you see those stinging nettles which grow outside this cave? You must pluck and weave them into eleven shirts for your brothers. This will free them from the spell, but there is one condition—while you are engaged on this work no word must pass your lips."

When Elise awoke in the morning she at once set to work to gather the stinging nettles, although they blistered her hands painfully. Then she trampled on the nettles with her naked feet and spun the green yarn. All day and all night she worked, for she could not rest until she had freed her brothers. The following day, when three shirts had been completed, Elise heard the sound of a hunting horn in the forest. The sound came nearer, and presently the King of that country, with his hunters, stood at the entrance to the cave. The King was so  struck by Elise's beauty that he wanted to make her his Queen. In spite of her tears and dumb protests (for, of course, she did not dare utter a word), she was carried off to the palace and dressed in the most beautiful and costly clothes. Now she looked more lovely than a vision and the King loved her even more tenderly than before.

Elise was grief-stricken for the fate of her brothers until one day she discovered in a cellar of the palace the three shirts which she had made and the bundle of green nettle yarn. One of the King's men had carried them from the cave. Every night after that she stole down to the cellar when the palace was asleep and worked all through the small hours on the remaining eight shirts.

One night, when she had finished the seventh shirt, the Archbishop saw her leave the cellar. Quietly he waited until she had returned to her own room and then he crept into the cellar and saw the shirts and the heap of nettle yarn. He went straight to the King and told him everything he had seen, whispering that the Queen must indeed be a witch and should be burnt at the stake.

The King wept bitterly, but since Elise did not utter a word in her own defence, he was powerless to save her. The guard took her away and locked her in the very cellar where the shirts and the nettles were, to await the day of execution. Elise wept for joy to find herself there and set feverishly to work upon the remaining four shirts. For two nights and a day she worked without ceasing, and just as she was finishing the last shirt the guard came to summon her. Grasping the eleven shirts, she was bundled into a cart and carried out through the palace gates. Just then eleven white swans appeared in the sky, and as they approached Elise recognised her brothers. They alighted on the cart beside her and quickly she threw the eleven shirts over them. Immediately they were changed into eleven handsome princes.

" Now I can speak! " cried Elise. " I am innocent."

" Yes, she is innocent! " said her eldest brother, and told the whole story.

The King cried for joy and took the fair Elise in his arms, happy to have his Queen back once more; and Elise was happy too, for now she had not only a very kind and handsome husband whom she loved, but she also had her eleven dear brothers restored to her.

BEAUTY
AND THE
BEAST

THERE was once a rich man who had three daughters. He was very fond of them, and gave them all the toys they wanted when they were little, and lovely clothes and jewels when they were growing up; but the two eldest girls were spoilt and never satisfied with any of his lovely presents.

The youngest daughter, who was called Beauty, was quite different. She was happy and good, and never asked him for anything, so, although he loved all three, the rich man could not help loving Beauty the best of all. She had long golden curls, skin like a pink rosebud, and a voice as sweet as a nightingale.

Now and then the father had to leave home, and he would always bring back a present for each of his daughters. So one day, as he was setting off, he said to them:

" What would you like me to bring you this time? "

The eldest girl clapped her hands, and said: " A pearl necklace for me, but it must be a long one, with a silver clasp."

The next one hugged her father, and said: "You know I have always wanted a golden bracelet, Father."

Then Beauty kissed her father, and said: "All I want is for you to come home safely," and both her sisters laughed.

"But I must bring you something," said the father.

"Then bring me a rose; I should like that very much,"

said Beauty, and her sisters laughed again and thought how silly she was not to ask for something better.

All went well until it was time for the rich man to return. He had bought the pearl necklace and the golden bracelet the two elder girls had asked for, and thought to himself: "I will leave the rose until I am nearly home, so that it will be fresh and sweet."

But as he travelled along, he was caught in a terrible storm. It grew so dark that he lost his way, and at last found himself outside a big house. Here he took shelter under some trees.

"Come inside!" called a voice. He could see no one, but the door was open, and he was glad to go in out of the rain.

Inside the house he found everything was of the richest, and there was a table laid with a splendid meal.

"Help yourself!" said the voice. "You may not see me because I do not wish it, but I shall be glad if you will stay here as long as you like."

"That is very kind," thought the father, and he was glad to stay the night in this grand house, even though he could see no one.

In the morning, when it was time for him to go, he looked again for someone to speak to, but there was nobody in sight.

"Then I must go without giving thanks," he thought.

It was not until he had reached the gates that the father remembered his promise to his youngest daughter, and then, as fine roses were growing there, he reached out his hand and picked one perfect bud, to take home to her. At once, a most terrible cry filled the air! The father looked up in alarm, and saw in front of him the most hideous man imaginable. This creature, who had the body of a man, but the head of a fearful beast, took him by the arm, and shouted: "How dare you rob me! I gave you the best I had, and you are still not content. You must even take my flowers!"

He would not let go until the poor father had promised to give the Beast anything in the world he asked for.

"You shall give me the very first thing you set your eyes on when you reach home," shouted the Beast in rage.

"Very well! I will do that, if I may still take the rose," agreed the father, and all the way home he thought to himself:

"It will be all right. I know it will be all right! One of the dogs is sure to rush out to meet me, and I can give the Beast that."

But he was wrong; for as soon as Beauty, who was watching, caught sight of him, she rushed out to kiss him.

"Have you brought my necklace?" called the eldest girl.

"And have you brought my bracelet?" demanded the other, but Beauty only thanked him sweetly for the rose, and led him indoors. The poor father thought how terrible it was that the kindest of his three girls should be given away to the Beast. But there was no help for it.

When he told Beauty about it she only said:

"It cannot be such a terrible beast. I will go with you gladly since he showed you kindness."

When Beauty and her father reached the grand house,

the Beast came out to meet them, and for a moment she felt like running away as fast as she could, but as soon as the Beast spoke and Beauty heard his kind voice, she turned to her father and implored him to go back to her sisters and tell them that all would be well.

Beauty now had everything of the finest, and the Beast brought her lovely jewels and clothes of silk and satin. All day long she had nothing to do but enjoy herself. But though Beauty was very afraid of the Beast, and glad when he kept out of her way, she knew that he was unhappy, and so she could not sing, or dance, or be glad.

One day the Beast gave her a magic mirror.

" I cannot let you go," he said; " but perhaps you will be happier if you can see your sisters and your father. Whenever you are feeling sad or lonely you have only to look in the mirror and you will see them as if they were here."

After that, Beauty used to sit by herself in the lovely garden, and gaze into the mirror, but one day she threw down the mirror and ran to the Beast, and said: " Please let me go! I have seen in the mirror that my father is ill."

" Very well," said the Beast; " but you must come back as soon as he is better, for I cannot live without you."

Beauty ran all the way home, and as soon as her father saw her he began to get better, and begged her never to leave him. Beauty was so happy that she forgot all about her promise to the Beast.

Weeks went by and no one ever spoke or even thought of the Beast. One day Beauty picked up the magic mirror, and looked into it, and she was so astonished at what she saw that she ran crying to her sisters.

"I must go," she cried. "The poor Beast is unhappy. I saw him through the mirror, and he was lying on the ground, and great tears rolled down his face."

"Who cares for an ugly beast, anyway!" said her sisters.

"I care!" said Beauty. "I care very much, for the Beast was always kind to me. Besides, I promised."

"Some promises are like pie-crust, made to be broken," said the eldest sister.

"I must go at once!" said Beauty. Her father was away from home, so there was no one to stop her.

When Beauty reached the grand house once more, she found the poor Beast just as she had seen him through the mirror, and now he was too weak even for tears. Beauty was so sad that she threw her arms around him and kissed him, saying: "Don't cry, poor Beast, don't cry! I will never leave you again."

The Beast sprang from the ground with a cry of delight, and, looking up at him, Beauty saw that he had completely changed! The hideous head had changed to a handsome one. The Beast had grown tall and straight and strong, like a young prince. He held out his arms and smiled.

"You have broken the spell," he cried. "The witch who changed me to a Beast said that only a kiss from a young girl could give me back my true shape!"

So Beauty and the Prince were married and lived happily for ever in the beautiful rose garden.

The SLEEPING BEAUTY

THE King and Queen invited all the most important fairies to the christening of their baby daughter, but they forgot the thirteenth fairy, and she was very angry indeed. She was so angry that she hid herself behind the curtains in the ballroom, where they were having the party, and listened.

She heard the other fairies, as they stooped over the baby's cradle, say, one after the other:

" She shall have happiness all her life! "

" She shall marry a handsome prince! "

" She shall be the loveliest Princess ever seen! "

" Her hair shall be like spun gold; her teeth like pearls! "

" Pah! " said the thirteenth fairy.

" What was that? " said the Queen.

"Nothing, my dear. Go on!" said the King graciously, to the next fairy in the queue.

The thirteenth fairy kept very still and listened. She was so angry that she lost count, and when she thought all the gifts had been given, out she pounced. . . .

"You forgot me, did you? Well, it will be the worse for you! Beautiful she may be, and good and all this, that and the other . . . but *my* gift will put an end to that. Ha! Ha! Ha! Listen to me, all of you . . ."

It was so quiet in the ballroom that you could have heard the flutter of a fairy's eyelash. The thirteenth fairy stood as straight and as tall as she could, and waved her magic wand. The baby began to cry, but nobody dared pick her up, or even rock the cradle. Everyone trembled with fear as the thirteenth fairy, in a loud and awful voice, declared:

"When the Princess is sixteen she shall die! She shall prick her finger and die at once; and that will be that!" and, with a horrid laugh, the thirteenth fairy disappeared in a puff of smoke.

Of course the party could not go on after that, and everyone turned sadly away.

"Wait!" said the Lilac Fairy. "I have not yet given *my* present to the little Princess."

The King and Queen hurried to the Lilac Fairy's side.

"It is not within my power to undo the wicked spell, but I can make it easier for you," she said. "The Princess, when she pricks her finger shall fall asleep for a hundred years. She may only be awakened by the kiss of a handsome prince."

"Thank you!" said the Queen.

"That's better!" agreed the King. "I suppose we shall go to sleep at the same time?"

" Naturally ! " said the Lilac Fairy, as she flew back to fairyland with the others.

" You know, my dear," said the King, " I think we ought to do something about this ourselves. Fairies are all very well . . . very good of them to give the child such splendid presents, but this spell . . ."

" But what can we do? " whispered the Queen.

" Use your common sense, my dear," said the King. " I have thought of a plan. If there are no needles or spindles in the kingdom, the Princess cannot possibly prick herself? "

So the King passed a new law, and after that there was not a spindle, nor a needle, nor a pin, to be found any-where, either in or out of the palace. Or so they thought, but the thirteenth fairy was too clever for them !

She flew back to the Palace on the day of the Princess's sixteenth birthday. All the lords and ladies of the Court were there, in their finest clothes, and there were several young princes from other countries, all very anxious to marry the young Princess, who had grown as lovely and as good as the other fairies had promised. The Princess herself was upstairs, fixing a sapphire crown on her golden hair.

" It would be easier if you had a pin, " said the thirteenth fairy, over the Princess's shoulder.

" A pin? What is that? " asked the Princess.

" Oh! " said the fairy, " you must know what a pin is like. It is sharp, like a needle . . . like the needle in a spinning-wheel. "

" But I have never seen or even heard of a spinning-wheel. I shall ask for one for my birthday present. "

"Will you come with me," said the Princess, "and tell my mother just what a spinning-wheel is like?"

"No need to trouble the Queen," said the thirteenth fairy. "I have kept one hidden away for you for this very day. Come with me and I will show you."

So the wicked fairy led the way and the young Princess followed her, along passages, and up stairs which she had never seen before. At last, at the top of a tall tower, they came to a little door set in the old grey stone.

"I must leave you here," said the fairy. "Knock on the door."

The Princess did as she was told, and at once the door creaked open and there stood an old, old woman, with silver hair under a snowy cap, and bright apple-red cheeks.

"Come in, my dear!" croaked the old woman, or rather, the thirteenth fairy, for of course it was she.

The Princess looked around her. The room was full of dust and cobwebs, and there, in the corner, stood something she had never seen before.

"You are looking at my spinning-wheel. It is the only one left, I believe," croaked the old woman.

"Please show me how to use it," said the Princess.

"Watch me, and you shall learn," said the old woman.

"Now, you shall try it yourself," she said.

"Thank you!" said the Princess. "It looks quite easy!" And she sat down.

But no sooner had she taken hold of it than she cried out: "Oh, how silly of me! I've pricked my finger!" And the very next second she had fallen asleep, there, all amongst the dust, in her wonderful party dress, and her bright little crown!

Down in the ballroom the King yawned, and said:
"It is getting late. Time the dancing began."

"But we can't start without . . ." said the Queen,
and the next instant she was fast asleep . . . so were
all the lords and ladies, the young princes, and all
the servants of the Palace. . . .

They fell asleep just as they were; the cook stirring a
pudding, the Princess's nurse folding clothes, the footman
holding the door for a latecomer. Even the horses in the
stables and the flies on the walls fell asleep. Inside the
Palace it seemed as though time stood still, and slowly
and softly year after year, the thin grey dust settled over
everything, but not a single speck of dust settled upon
the Princess. She remained as lovely as ever, right
through a hundred years. . . .

Outside the Palace a hedge of brambles sprang up; so
thick and high that no one knew what lay behind it.

One day a young prince rode by on a white horse, and stopped in amazement. "This is the place I have dreamed of!" he cried. "If I can get through this hedge, I shall find the most beautiful Princess in the world."

The Prince took his sword, and slashed at the brambles until he had cleared a pathway.

"Just like my dream!" he said, when he passed the sleeping courtiers; and he wasted no time, but went on until he came to the narrow stairway, and the little door in the grey stone. There he found the Princess asleep. He stooped over and kissed her, and at once she awoke.

"I have waited a long time for you," she said, and they both laughed and ran downstairs to the others.

The King rubbed the dust from his eyes. "I fell asleep," he yawned. "Dear me, this is the day you choose your prince!" he said, smiling at his daughter.

"I have chosen already!" said the little Princess.

HANSEL AND GRETEL

HANSEL and Gretel lived with their father, who was a woodcutter, in a little hut at the edge of a forest. For a long time they were very happy. They would go off with their father in the early morning and stay near him while he worked. The two children collected berries and nuts and mushrooms, or picked bunches of wild flowers. Gretel was clever at weaving and she made little baskets from dried grasses.

But all this was changed when their father married again, for their stepmother was cruel, and thought nothing the children did was right. She was a greedy woman, too, and began to complain and to say that there was not enough food, and that the children must go. One night, as he lay awake in his little bed, Hansel heard his father sadly agree to take the children into the forest and lose them. Hansel waited until the very early

morning, and then, before the others were awake, he crept out of the little hut and filled his pockets with small white pebbles.

That day, when they were deep in the forest, the father said, " You must wait here until I come back. "

The children waited until it grew dark and cold, and at last Gretel said, " He must have forgotten all about us. "

Then Hansel told her of all that his stepmother had said.

" But never mind! " said Hansel. " I have left a trail of little white pebbles along the way we came, and as soon as the moon is up, we shall be able to find our way home. "

When the horrid stepmother opened the door of the hut, there were the two children, waiting to come in. She smiled and pretended to be pleased to see them, and

only scolded them for straying away from their father.

The next night Hansel again heard his father agree to take the children with him, and to lose them.

" Take them deeper into the wood this time," scolded the woman. " We cannot go on feeding them for ever. They must find their own way in the world."

Sadly the father did as he had promised, and they walked until the two children were weary and could go no farther. Then the father made a splendid bonfire, and the children lay down under a tree and were soon fast asleep. When they awoke the fire was out and the man was already miles away.

" Never mind!" said Hansel. " We shall be able to find our way, for although the door was locked and I could not go out to collect pebbles, I had some crusts in my pocket, and I have made a trail with them."

It was already early morning, and the two children

set off, hand in hand; but there were no crumbs left, for the birds had flown down and eaten them.

Gretel began to cry, but Hansel said, " Look, Gretel! Do you see the smoke rising above those trees? There must be a woodman's hut there. We will go and ask for food."

The children followed the direction of the smoke and presently found themselves in a little clearing, and there stood a dear little house!

Hansel and Gretel ran up to it, and were just going to knock when they saw that the door was made of chocolate.

" We need not be hungry any more," said Gretel.

" Look! " said Hansel. " The walls of the house are made of gingerbread, and the window-frames are barley sugar! " And both the children burst out laughing.

Out popped a little old woman from the door.

"What jolly children!" she said. "Come in, my dears, there are more good things inside."

Happily Hansel and Gretel followed her into the little house. The old woman set the table and gave them a good meal. She seemed to have a store of everything children like, in her cupboards, and after they had eaten the old woman led them upstairs into a pretty bedroom and said: "You shall rest here, my dears, and when you are ready we will have another meal."

After a few days of such kindness, and such good food, Hansel and Gretel began to grow quite plump.

One morning, Gretel woke to find that Hansel's bed was empty.

"Where is my brother?" she asked the old woman.

"Get on with your work! I shall want a great heap of firewood, for I must make the oven nice and hot," said the old woman.

When Gretel was outside the cottage she heard Hansel crying, and looking around, she found him tied up in the hen-house. She told Hansel that the old woman had given orders for the oven to be made ready.

Hansel said to his sister: " You must help the old woman. Do not say that you have found me, but do as she asks."

Then Gretel bent down, in case the old woman was somewhere nearby, and Hansel told her what to do.

Gretel ran off, and all day long she collected wood!

Every now and then she would say to the old woman:

" I do wonder where Hansel can have got to? " and the old woman would chuckle as if she had a splendid secret, but she did not reply.

Towards evening, when Gretel was almost too tired to work any longer, and the fire was so strong and bright that the heat in the little kitchen was unbearable, the old woman said: " Good! It is hot enough now. The oven is ready."

" Are you going to roast a goose? " asked Gretel.

" Yes, my dear, a nice, plump, little goose," laughed the old woman.

" But surely," said Gretel, " you never mean to put a goose in the oven without finding out first whether the heat is too little or too much? You might scorch it and then your supper would be spoilt."

" H'm! " said the old woman. " It is quite a clever child! I should never have thought of that! " and she opened the oven door and popped her head inside, just to see whether or not it was the right heat.

Quick as lightning, Gretel seized the old woman, and with one tremendous heave she thrust her inside the oven and slammed the door. Then she ran out to Hansel and set him free.

" Let us run into the wood and hide ! " said Hansel.

" But we cannot leave the old woman in the oven ! " said Gretel.

" She is cruel, like a bad witch," said Hansel; but Gretel led him back to the kitchen, where the old woman was crying and begging to be let out.

" Will you be good, for always and always? " asked Gretel.

" I *will* be good for always and always ! " said the old woman.

" Will you never be unkind to any child who may knock on the door? " asked Hansel.

" Never—never—never ! " sobbed the old woman.

" Then if I may have your magic stick you shall come out," asked Hansel.

" Take it ! " said the old woman. " It is behind the

door. The stick will obey you always, and it will turn all that it touches into nice things to eat; toffee or sponge-cake, gingerbread or chocolate, just as you wish."

So Gretel unlatched the oven door, and Hansel helped the old woman out, and after that she was no trouble.

Sometimes Hansel would say to the stick: "Fetch my father here!" and the stick would run out, and almost at once the woodcutter would knock on the door, and say: "Do Hansel and Gretel live in this little house?"

Then they would have a lovely day together; but, of course, neither Hansel nor Gretel ever invited the step-mother!

Puss in Boots

THERE was once a cat who knew exactly what he wanted: a comfortable home, a warm place by the fire, and plenty of good food without the trouble of hunting for it.

But this cat was also very fond of his master, who had none of these things. He was a young and handsome man, who wandered from place to place in search of work, but without much luck. The cat soon saw that he would have to be the clever one, so he said:

"If you will find me a sack and a strong pair of boots I will catch something good for our dinners."

"Very well, Puss," said the young man, and he spent his last shillings on an elegant pair of boots for the cat. The cat was gone a long time, but at last he returned with a rabbit.

" What ! " said his master. " Have you been away so long, and caught only this small creature ? "

" Indeed, no ! " purred the cat. " I have been to the Palace, and spoken to the King. I gave him the rest of the rabbits and told him how to have them cooked for dinner."

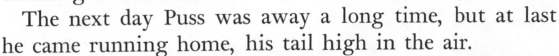

His master laughed, and stroked the cat softly, never thinking it was true.

The next day Puss was away a long time, but at last he came running home, his tail high in the air.

" Where have you been this time, Puss? " laughed his master. " I suppose you have been visiting the King again ? "

" Throw off your clothes and dive into the river," said the cat. " There's no time to lose ! "

" Whatever next ! " laughed the young man.

" Do as I say ! " urged Puss. " I promise it will bring good fortune."

Of course his master did not believe a word, but as it was a hot day, and the water looked cool and refreshing, he obeyed. When his master was in the water, the cat hid his shabby clothes and ran off.

" Whatever next ! " said the man, but he was even

more surprised when a fine carriage appeared, driven by coach-
men, and out of the coach
jumped his friend the cat!

" There is my master, the
Duke of Carabas, bathing in the
river, Your Majesty," announced
the cat.

" The one who sent me those
fine rabbits yesterday, and the pheasants to-day? "
inquired the King.

" I should like to meet the Duke, too," said his daughter,
the Princess.

" So you shall, my dear, so you shall! " said the King.
The cat ran to his master and whispered: " Stay where
you are! You just leave this to me! " The young man
was too astonished to speak.

" A terrible thing has happened," said the cat, bowing

low before the King. "Some thieves have run off with my master's clothes while he was in the river!"

"Most unfortunate! Most unfortunate!" remarked the King, and he at once sent one of his servants riding back to the Palace to fetch a handsome suit.

"You have heard of the Duke of Carabas, I'm sure," said the cat proudly when his master had dressed.

"Of course! Of course! Delighted to meet you, my dear fellow!" said the King. "You must come and dine with us at the Palace, and tell me whether my cook has properly understood your cat's recipes. A very clever cat I must say."

"Yes!" said the young man, who had eyes only for the Princess.

"Yes, indeed!" said the Princess, who had eyes only for the young man.

"Then I will meet you here later," said the cat, who was already busy with other plans for his master's future, and for his own place by the warm hearth-side.

The cat ran off to a splendid castle, and mewed and mewed at the door until it was opened.

"What do you want?" growled the fierce ogre who lived there.

"A warm place by the fire."

" And what will you give me? " demanded the ogre.

" I will catch mice for you," said Puss.

" There are no mice," said the ogre, and he was just going to shut the front door, when the cat ran in, between his legs, and saw for himself that it was a very fine place indeed, and just what he was looking for.

" Can you work magic? " he said to the ogre, purring, and rubbing against him.

" Magic! " roared the ogre. " I should think I can! Why I could turn myself into a lion."

" Could you, indeed," purred Puss. " That is clever, but I think it would be cleverer still if anyone as big and strong as you could turn himself into something small . . . a mouse for instance."

" I suppose you think I'm not quite clever enough for that, eh? " roared the ogre. " Well, I'll show you! "

And the next moment the ogre had vanished, and there, instead, was a tiny brown mouse; but of course it was not there the moment after that, for the cat, who was waiting for this to happen, caught it and gobbled it up!

Then Puss ran back to the place where he had left his master, and waited, quietly purring to himself, until the Royal carriage appeared.

" Ah, there you are! " said the young man.

" Everything is ready and waiting," announced Puss.

The cat sprang into the carriage and directed the way.

" This is the castle of the Duke of Carabas," he announced proudly, as they came to the ogre's estate. His master was too astonished to speak, and the King and the Princess were surprised too, when they entered and saw the richness of the place.

As for Puss, he went straight to the fireside, and curled himself into a tight, round ball. He knew that he had earned his place on the hearth, and need never go hunting again!

The FROG PRINCE

ONCE upon a time, a little Princess with two long braids of golden hair lived in a castle with her father, the King, and her mother, the Queen. She had no brothers nor sisters, but when she had finished her lessons she would play quite happily by herself in the gardens of the castle. Her favourite toy was a golden ball that glittered as she tossed it into the air. When she threw it into a hedge or lost it in a bed of flowers, one of the gardeners would find it for her.

One hot day, the Princess ran out of the castle garden into the cool green forest, carrying her golden ball in her hand. She came to a mossy glade where a huge lime tree threw its shade, and near the lime tree lay a great pool with the broad leaves and waxen cups of water-lilies floating on its water. The Princess sat down under the lime tree and started tossing her golden ball into the air. She tossed and caught it six times over, but the seventh time she did not catch it. The golden ball fell, splash, into the pool.

The Princess ran to the edge of the pool and began to cry. " My golden ball ! " she wept. " It has sunk to the bottom ! I shall never see it again ! "

" Don't cry, Princess," croaked a sad voice. " What will you give me if I fetch your ball from the bottom of the pool ? "

The Princess looked round in all directions, but she saw nobody except a big green frog sitting on a broad water-lily leaf and staring at her with small bright eyes.

" Will you fetch my ball ? " she cried.

" Yes, I will dive to the bottom of the pool and bring you your golden ball if you promise to give me what I ask," answered the frog.

" Oh, I will give you anything you ask ! " cried the Princess. " I will drop a silver penny into the pool for you, or even my pearl ring ! "

" I have no use for silver pennies or jewels," croaked the frog. " Even your little golden crown would be worth nothing to me. But let me be your companion ! Promise me that I can sit at your table, eat from your crystal plate, drink from your silver goblet, and sleep on your silk pillow. Then I will dive down into the water and find your golden ball."

" I promise !" said the Princess, and at once heard, Splash ! Splash ! and saw bubbles on the water as the frog dived off the leaf of the water-lily into the pool.

" What a silly old frog to ask such foolish things !" she said to herself, tossing her golden plaits. But she smiled for joy when she heard another splash and saw the frog hop back on the leaf with the golden ball in his mouth. He threw the ball on the grass near her feet and without even saying Thank You ! the Princess picked it up and ran away home.

" Wait for me !" croaked a sad voice behind her. " I cannot run like you, I can only hop !" But the Princess took no notice and ran back to the castle as fast as she could.

" Foolish old frog !" she said to herself. " He can

go back to his pool and splash and croak all day long. I shan't see him again."

She told nobody about losing her golden ball.

That night the Princess sat at supper with the King and Queen and the ladies and gentlemen of the Court. The candles were all lit in the tall silver candlesticks and the candlelight shone on silver dishes and on the ladies' jewels. In a gallery, the musicians made soft music. But when the music stopped for a few minutes, the Princess

raised her head and looked towards the door, as if she were listening to something. Everybody else stopped talking and listened too.

It was only a soft little sound they heard through the door. A sound like " Hop—hop—hop ! " coming nearer and nearer up the marble staircase. The Princess turned pale. " Hop—hop—hop " they heard, and a minute later there came a soft little tap on the door.

> " *Lovely Princess,*
> *Open to me.*"

croaked a voice outside.

" Who can it be ? " asked the King in surprise. " Go and see, my dear."

The Princess went slowly to the door, opened it about half an inch, looked through, and shut the door again very quickly.

" Who was it ? " asked the King.

" Only an ugly frog," answered the Princess, trying to smile.

" A frog ! " exclaimed the King, more surprised than ever. " Whatever can he want ? "

But even as he spoke they heard another tap on the door and the frog's voice croaked :

> " *Don't you remember*
> *The promise you made,*
> *When you lost your toy*
> *In the lime tree's shade?* "

" What is he talking about ? " asked the King.

" Well, you see," said the Princess, " I lost my golden ball in the pool and the frog brought it back to me. I promised him he should be my companion, so he followed me home. I will tell somebody to throw him downstairs, the ugly creature."

The King looked severely at the Princess.

" Whatever promise you made, you must keep it," he said. " Even a promise to an ugly frog."

Then the Princess, looking quite sulky, went to open the door. The frog came in, hop—hop—hop ! over the carpet, hop—hop—hop ! right up to the Princess's chair.

" I can't reach the table," he croaked. "Lift me, Princess."

Pouting, the Princess set the ugly frog on the linen table-cloth where he sat blinking his sad, small eyes at the candlelight.

" Give me my supper," he croaked.

" There isn't a plate," said the Princess.

" But Princess," said the frog, " have you forgotten ? You promised I should eat off your own crystal plate."

The King looked sternly at the Princess, so she pushed her beautiful crystal plate nearer the ugly frog, who ate some of her supper. The Princess ate nothing, but she picked up her goblet of silver to sip some wine.

" Give me a drink," croaked the frog.

" You can drink water from a saucer," said the Princess.

" Princess, have you forgotten ? " asked the frog. " You promised I should drink from your own silver goblet."

So the poor Princess, look-ing more sulky than ever, passed her silver goblet to the frog who took several sips of wine. Then he sighed, looked round with his sad, beady eyes, and croaked :

" Where is your bed ? I am tired."

"Take him upstairs to rest," said the King severely. "He helped you when you were in trouble, so you must keep the promise you made him."

The Princess shivered at the very thought of the ugly frog hopping into her bedroom, but she dared not disobey the King.

" You can hop up the stairs, I will find you a room," she said to the frog.

The frog closed his eyes sleepily.

" You must carry me, I am too tired to hop any farther. And don't forget you promised I should sleep on your own silk pillow."

So the Princess had to pick up the frog in her fingers and carry him up another flight of stairs to her bedroom where she put him in a dark corner hoping he would go to sleep. Tired and hungry, she herself got into her little white bed and laid her head down on the silk pillow. In a few minutes she fell asleep.

Hop—hop—hop! Hop—hop—hop! A soft little noise woke the Princess. There sat the ugly frog in the middle of the floor. She could see him quite plainly in the rays of moonlight that fell through her window.

"Princess," croaked the frog. "Remember your promise. Let me sleep on your silk pillow."

Then the Princess flew into a temper and cried:

"You've eaten from my crystal plate, you've drunk from my silver goblet. But I will not let an ugly—cold—green—frog sleep on my silk pillow! Go and sleep in the fountain in the garden! Better still, go back to your pool!"

She got out of bed, picked up the poor frog, leaned out of the window, and dropped him on the lawn below.

"Good-bye, ugly frog!" she said.

Even as she spoke the ugly frog vanished. The Princess rubbed her eyes thinking she must be dreaming, for now a tall and handsome Prince smiled up at her as she leaned from her window in the moonlight.

" Princess," he said, " you have broken the spell of an evil witch who changed me into a frog. My carriage and six white horses are waiting at the castle gates."

So the Princess became the bride of the Frog Prince and drove away with him into his own country.

GOLDILOCKS and the THREE BEARS

THERE was once a little girl called Goldilocks who lived in a house near a wood with her mother and father. She was called Goldilocks because she had the most beautiful long hair which fell to her waist in soft curls. She had big blue eyes, a turned-up nose and rosy-red lips.

One warm summer's day Goldilocks went into the woods to gather some flowers. Her mother and father had often warned her not to stray too far from home in case she got lost, and usually Goldilocks stayed near her own garden. But this day she was feeling adventurous and a little bit naughty, so she decided to explore the woods. She wandered among the trees for a while and, just when she was beginning to realise that she was lost, she came upon a pretty cottage standing in a clearing.

" What a dear little house! " said Goldilocks. " I have never seen it before. I wonder who lives there? "

She was a very curious little girl so she went up to the house and knocked at the door. No one came. She opened the door and went in. In the first room she came to she saw three bowls of porridge set on the table. There was a great big bowl, a medium-sized bowl and a tiny little bowl. The porridge smelled so good that it made Goldilocks feel quite hungry. She tried the porridge in the great big bowl but it was too hot. She tried the porridge in the medium-sized bowl but it was too cold. Then she tried the porridge in the tiny little bowl and it was just right, so she ate it all up.

When she had finished she noticed that in front of the fire stood three chairs, a large chair, a medium-sized chair and a tiny little chair.

Goldilocks sat in the large one but it was too hard. She tried the middle one but it was too soft. But the little

chair was just right so Goldilocks sat down in it until—*bang*—the bottom of the chair fell out and she landed on the floor.

"I wonder what is upstairs," thought Goldilocks as she picked herself off the floor. "I'll go up and see."

In the bedroom upstairs were three beds—an enormous bed, a medium-sized bed and a tiny little bed. The biggest bed was too hard and the middle bed was too soft, but the tiny little bed was just right.

Goldilocks felt very sleepy and she lay down on it. It was so comfortable that soon she fell fast asleep.

By-and-by the owners of the cottage came home. They were three bears—a Daddy Bear, a Mummy Bear and a Baby Bear. They had been shopping at a nearby village and now they were feeling very tired and hungry. They were looking forward to eating their porridge and to having a nice long rest. But as soon as they came in, they noticed that things weren't exactly as they had left them and that someone had been in their house.

In the biggest bowl of porridge there was a spoon, and the medium-sized bowl had finger-marks all over it.

" Who's been eating *my* porridge? " growled Daddy Bear.

" Who's been eating *my* porridge? " cried Mummy Bear.

" And who's been eating *my* porridge? " squeaked Baby Bear, " and has eaten it all up! "

Then the Bear family noticed something wrong with

their fireside chairs. The biggest chair was out of position and a cushion from the medium-sized chair lay on the floor.

"Who's been sitting in *my* chair?" growled Daddy Bear.

"Who's been sitting in *my* chair?" cried Mummy Bear.

"And who's been sitting on *my* chair?" squeaked Baby Bear. "They've broken it to pieces!"

Then the bears decided to go upstairs to look around because they thought that thieves had been in their house. They went into the bedroom and right away they noticed that the biggest bed was all rumpled, and the sheets and blankets on the

medium-sized bed were very untidy. They *were* annoyed.

" Who's been lying on *my* bed? " growled Daddy Bear.

" Who's been lying on *my* bed? " cried Mummy Bear.

" And who's been lying on *my* bed? " squeaked Baby Bear. " And look—she's still there! It's a little girl! "

At the sound of their voices Goldilocks woke up with a start. What a fright she had to see the three bears looking down on her!

But they were kind bears although they looked so fierce and when Goldilocks said she was sorry to have gone into their house, they forgave her. They said she could come back and see them often and Goldilocks was very pleased.

Then Daddy Bear took Goldilocks home, while Mummy Bear and Baby Bear stood at the cottage door waving good-bye to her.